FOR GLORIA, MADELEINE, ROSIE, AND GILBERT

FIRST NORTH AMERICA EDITION PUBLISHED IN 2013 BY BOXER BOOKS LIMITED.
FIRST PUBLISHED IN GREAT BRITAIN IN 2013 BY BOXER BOOKS LIMITED.
WWW.BOXERBOOKS.COM

TEXT AND ILLUSTRATIONS COPYRIGHT © 2013 ALGY CRAIG HALL

THE RIGHT OF ALGY CRAIG HALL TO BE IDENTIFIED AS THE AUTHOR AND
ILLUSTRATOR OF THIS WORK HAS BEEN ASSERTED BY HIM
IN ACCORDANCE WITH THE COPYRIGHT, DESIGNS AND PATENTS ACT, 1988.

THE ILLUSTRATIONS WERE PREPARED USING CHARCOAL AND DIGITAL COLOR
THE TEXT IS SET IN KEENER AND HELVETICA

ISBN 978-1-907967-50-4

1 3 5 7 9 10 8 6 4 2

PRINTED IN SINGAPORE

ALL OF OUR PAPERS ARE SOURCED FROM MANAGED FORESTS AND RENEWABLE RESOURCES.

DINO BITES!

ALGY CRAIG HALL

BOXER BOOKS

This is the dinosaur looking for lunch.

This is the lunch looking for a snack.

This is the snack looking for a bite.

Dinosaur.

Lunch.

Snack.

Bite.

Bite!

Cru

nch!

But the bite buzzed.

The snack hopped.

The lunch wriggled.